Published by **Lion Children's Books**
www.lionhudson.com
Part of the SPCK Group
SPCK, 36 Causton Street, London, SW1P 4ST

ISBN 978 0 7459 7985 4

Unabridged text first published in 1978
First abridged edition 2006
This mini edition April 2022

All rights reserved

A catalogue record for this book is available
from the British Library

Printed and bound in China, January 2022, LH54

To Micah and the
next generation M.D.

To my very best friend
Shannon with love G.H.

Meryl
Doney

ILLUSTRATED BY

Gaby
Hansen

The Very Worried Sparrow

LION
CHILDREN'S

There was once a Very Worried Sparrow.
All the other baby birds looked up at the bright
blue sky and sang, 'Cheep, cheep! Cheep, cheep!'
    But not the Very Worried Sparrow. 'Meep, meep,'
he said in a very little voice.
    The first thing he worried about was food.

'Oh dear!' he thought. 'I'm so hungry.
Whatever am I going to eat?'
    Suddenly, there was Mother, with a fat,
juicy caterpillar for each baby bird.

One day, Father gathered the
little sparrows around him.

'I think it is time you learned to fly,'
he said. 'Open your wings and flap.'

'Wheeeeeee, this is lovely,'
called the sparrows.

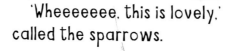

'Meep, meep,' said the Very Worried Sparrow. 'I don't dare.'

He was so scared he lost his balance, toppled off the branch... flipped... and flapped... and flew!

When the sun went down. Father sparrow gathered his family together. warm and snug in the nest.

He told them wonderful stories of long ago and far away:

of the Great Father who made the world and everything in it:

of how the day begins, and where the wind comes from, and all the little things that every creature knows.

The young birds listened with bright eyes.

But the Very Worried Sparrow peered out into the darkness. 'Meep,' he said, 'oh dear!'

When summer came, the Very Worried Sparrow
felt just a little braver. He set off with his brothers
and sisters to look for seeds in the field.

SWOOSH!

The terrible sparrowhawk
came diving down. The Very
Worried Sparrow closed his
eyes tight and waited,
too scared to move.

But when he opened
them, he saw the
sparrowhawk flying away.

'Meep, meep,' said the Very Worried
Sparrow. 'I'm going home.' And he flew
to the nest as fast as he could.

The autumn winds blew and
the trees shed their leaves.
Then the snow fell, covering
the ground in a soft layer of
sparkling white. The sparrows
thought it was wonderful.

   The Very Worried Sparrow peered about him.
'The snow has covered up all the food,' he said.
'And where will we find water to drink?'

But each morning children scattered seeds on the path and broke the ice that glazed the pond. The sparrows had plenty to eat and drink all through the winter.

Spring came and the sparrows twittered with excitement.
'It's nesting time.' they said.

They swooped and sang with all the other sparrows.

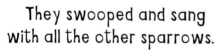

Soon pairs of birds were darting away. looking for safe places to build their nests.

'Meep, meep,' said the Very Worried Sparrow,
his head drooping. 'I'm all alone.'

The branch bounced as a little sparrow
fluttered closer.

'Cheep,' she said shyly.

'Meep, meep,' said the Very Worried Sparrow.
'Will you be my friend?'

'Oh yes!' she said happily.

'I know a good place for a nest,' she said.
'Come and see.'

Together they flew to a lovely apple tree.
'Meep, meep,' said the Very Worried Sparrow.
'It's lovely. But I expect other birds have found
it already.'

'It's a safe place just for us,' chirruped his mate.
'Come on!'

Before long, the shy sparrow was sitting
in the nest. Under her warm feathers were
four speckled eggs.

'Meep, meep,' said the Very Worried Sparrow.
'Soon I'll have a family to worry about.'
    Far below, in the grass, a cat was prowling.
    High above, a sparrowhawk drifted on the wind.

The Very Worried Sparrow was looking very,
very… worried!

 'Roo coo. What's the matter?' asked a gentle voice.

 It was the turtledove with soft white feathers.

 'I'm so worried,' wept the sparrow.

'Roo coo,' said the dove.
'Don't you know the stories of the Great Father
who made us all and who cares about every sparrow?'
'Meep, meep,' said the Very Worried Sparrow.
'I was so worried, I didn't listen.'

So, as the sun went down, the dove gathered all the birds around her, and told the stories of long ago and far away:

of the Great Father who made the world and everything in it:

of how the day begins, and where the wind comes from, and all the little things that every creature knows.

She spoke of the seasons and the years, of how things grow and new life comes. She told how the Great Father knows each creature and its time on the earth.

The next day, the whole world sparkled
in the morning light.

'Tock, tock, tock.' A tiny sound came from
each of the eggs, and soon four new baby
sparrows hatched in the cosy nest.

Then the Very Worried Sparrow...smiled!

'I can't wait to see them,' he said.
'We can watch them grow and teach
them to fly. And I will tell them about the Great Father
who made the world and everything in it, and who
knows each sparrow. They won't have to worry
for a single day.'
Then the Very Worried Sparrow flew up into
the blue sky.
'Cheep, cheep,' he sang, 'CHEEP, CHEEP, CHEEP,'
loud enough to burst with happiness.